This book is dedicated to my children
Shannon, Beth, Ryan and James who inspired the
writing of this story and my husband, Bruce,
who encouraged me to publish this work.

Acknowledgement:

To Paul Brittenham whose illustrations
brought my story to life.

About the author:

Laura Hotchkiss authored
The Moral of the Stories Series
from the inspiration of her four children.
Her education includes a BA from the
University of California, San Diego
and Doctorate from combined study at
Dartmouth and Brown. She and her husband
currently reside in the Northwest United States.

About the illustrator:

Paul Brittenham lives and works in a log cabin
that he, his wife and three girls built in the
Finger Lakes region of New York State.
Visit his gallery at paulbrittenham.com

Why Not Walnut?

by Laura Hotchkiss

illustrations by Paul Brittenham

Wally, the walnut, wanted it all. "I want to reach out and touch the sky. I want to make history. I want a happy family."

But the other walnuts on the tree told him he was just a dreamer; they would say "Stop kidding yourself, you will just be someone's dinner."

It was true. Wally grew on a tree in a walnut grove. He was grown to be sold as food, but Wally just couldn't believe that was his destiny. He would say to them, "Why not?"

Of course they would laugh and say "You silly nut."

Early one cool crisp morning while Wally was just hanging out dreaming of his future, he was startled awake to a strange noise. The noise kept getting louder and louder.

"Oh no! The harvesting machine!" The machine was going from tree to tree shaking the walnuts down to be swept up and taken away. Wally shook in fear, so hard that he fell before the machine came to his tree. "Maybe I can escape," he thought, "but how?"

Suddenly, a squirrel took Wally in its mouth and carried him away.

"Oh, this is wonderful!" he thought, until he realized that he might be the squirrel's dinner. Again Wally shook in fear, so hard that the squirrel dropped him.

Wally fell to the ground, rolled down a bank into the stream below. He was caught in the current and began floating away.

Where was he going? Well, at least he wasn't being eaten.

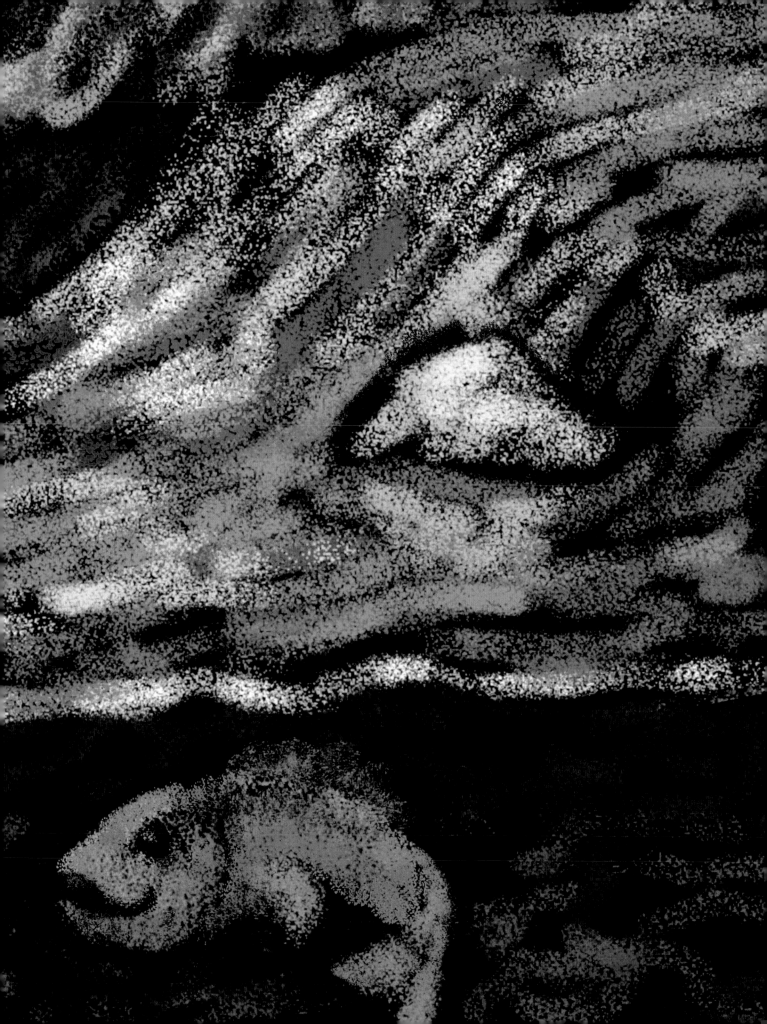

Wally was getting used to the leisurely ride which took him swirling in eddies and down small waterfalls. He liked bobbing up and down. It was actually kind of fun, until all of a sudden he was scooped out of the water. A little girl named Caroline picked him up.

"What is this?" she asked her brother Jack.

Jack took a look. He did not know. "Looks like some kind of seed," he said.

Jack threw Wally through the air. Wally felt a sudden stop.

"Ha, caught it!" shouted Peter.

"What is it?" asked Jack.

Peter replied, "I don't know, but it makes a good ball!"

Before he knew it, Wally was being thrown back and forth and back and forth through the air. "When is this ever going to stop?"

It wasn't until at long last Wally heard, "Hey, that's mine, give it back!" Caroline caught Wally and he finally felt safe in her warm hands.

Caroline ran into the house. "Mommy, Mommy, look what I found!"

Caroline's Mom looked at Wally. "Oh, that is a walnut."

Caroline looked at her Mom. "I thought walnuts were brown and bumpy; this is green and smooth."

Caroline's Mom explained: "A walnut has an outer husk, like corn, then a hard shell inside. Inside the hard shell is the nut."

"Would you like to eat it?"

Wally thought he was going to faint hearing those words. Luckily Caroline replied, "No, I want to keep it, not eat it!"

"OKAY" said her mother.

"Whew!" thought Wally.

Caroline brought Wally upstairs to her room. "I am going to make you into a doll!"

First Caroline drew a happy face on Wally. Next she glued yarn to his head for hair and gave him pigtails. Using two popsicle sticks she gave him a body and arms. The finishing touch was a lovely pink dress with yellow polka dots.

Caroline raced down the stairs to show her Mom.

"Mom, look what I did!"

With a big smile her Mom replied, "Very creative!"

Caroline played with Wally day after day. "So this is what it is like to have a family" thought Wally. Wally was so very happy. But, like many things in life, change happens. For Wally, the change happened the week before Christmas.

The family was downstairs having a wonderful evening of fun decorating the house and Christmas tree when Wally overheard Peter speaking. "Look what I found in this box!"

Dad went over to look. "Careful, that is a family heirloom from your great grandparents. It is a nutcracker from Germany."

"Let's try it!" said Peter. The boys were disappointed to hear Dad say they didn't have any nuts to crack.

Then Jack had a great thought. "Caroline does!"

Jack and Peter looked at each other and both took off running up the stairs. Peter grabbed Wally and ran back downstairs.

"That's mine!" shouted Caroline. Peter threw Wally to Jack. Caroline ran over and started to grab Wally from Jack. Dad was shouting break it up as Mom walked in the front door.

Just as Jack let go, the doll Caroline had made fell apart. Wally, with the yarn on his head and smile on his face rolled out the front door.

Caroline then ran out the front door after Wally. It was dark and cold outside. The wind was blowing and snow was falling fast. She couldn't see Wally.

Her Mom turned on the porch light. Together they looked but couldn't find him.

Finally, Caroline's Mom said, "Let's go inside, we can try again later." Wally then heard soft crying from inside the house.

Time passed and Wally stayed put, but he felt something was happening.

Peter was outside. "When you finish pulling the weeds we will go to the pool," he heard his Mom say from inside the house.

Caroline stepped outside. "Can I help?" she asked.

"Sure," said Peter and he handed her some gloves. The kids were working side by side making their way closer to Wally.

"Is this a weed?" asked Caroline.

"No, I don't think so," said Peter. "Hey, Dad! What is this?" he shouted.

Dad came over, looked down, and said "I believe that is a young walnut tree. How did it get here?"

Caroline instantly knew that was her walnut. It was her tree. She shouted for joy, and of course Wally was there to stay. Caroline made a small rock garden around Wally and tended to him with water and fertilizer. He grew strong under her watchful eye.

As years passed, Wally grew taller. He reached for the sky and basked in the warmth of the sun. He heard many compliments as people walked by him to go to the house. "Such a nice tree!" and "Doesn't this shade feel good?"

When he was strong enough, a swing was hung from his branches. He loved the lazy days with the kids, even the grownups, relaxing under his canopy.

Two of his dreams had come true. He had his family and he had reached out and touched the sky.

Wally no longer cared about his other dream, he was happy. But, like many things in life, change happens.

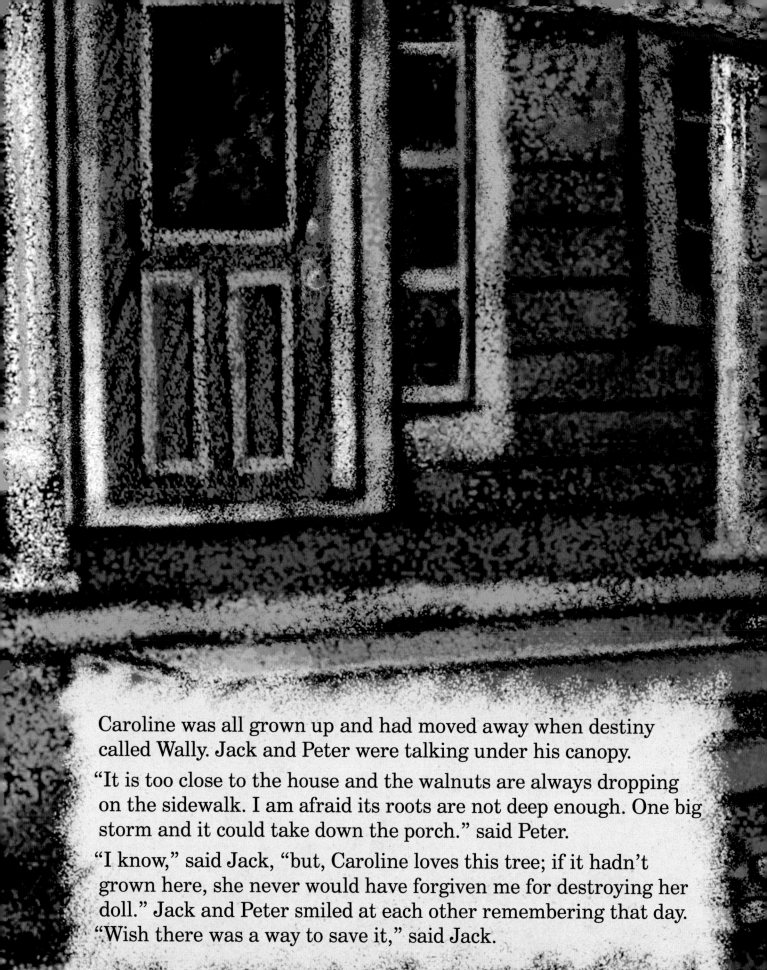

Caroline was all grown up and had moved away when destiny called Wally. Jack and Peter were talking under his canopy.

"It is too close to the house and the walnuts are always dropping on the sidewalk. I am afraid its roots are not deep enough. One big storm and it could take down the porch." said Peter.

"I know," said Jack, "but, Caroline loves this tree; if it hadn't grown here, she never would have forgiven me for destroying her doll." Jack and Peter smiled at each other remembering that day. "Wish there was a way to save it," said Jack.

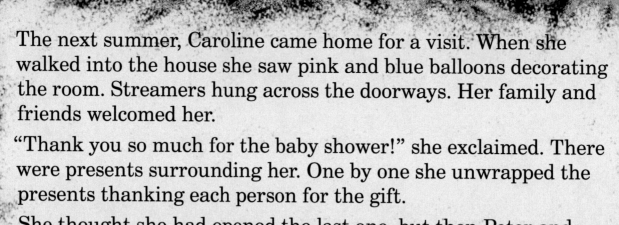

The next summer, Caroline came home for a visit. When she walked into the house she saw pink and blue balloons decorating the room. Streamers hung across the doorways. Her family and friends welcomed her.

"Thank you so much for the baby shower!" she exclaimed. There were presents surrounding her. One by one she unwrapped the presents thanking each person for the gift.

She thought she had opened the last one, but then Peter and Jack smiled and announced there was one more in the next room.

As she walked into the room, she saw a beautiful rocking chair with a big red bow. "This is exquisite, the most beautiful wood I have ever seen!"

"Try it" said Jack and Peter. Caroline sat down on the beautiful rocker and rocked back and forth.

It was then that she realized. "Is this my walnut?"

"Yes," Peter replied.

"There was too much history to just cut down that walnut tree and walk away. Jack and I made the rocker for you so that you can remember us as kids and create more memories with your baby. It will be a new family heirloom."

Wally was so very happy, his dreams had all come true.
He had a family, he had reached out to the sky and now
would make history.

Moral of the Story:
When you are told that your dreams will never come true,
just say "Why not?"

Made in the USA
Middletown, DE
29 November 2022

16410055R00024